Adult

MAD LIBS®

World's Greatest Word Game

DYSFUNCTIONAL FAMILY THERAPY MAD LIBS

By Roger Price and Leonard Stern

PSS!
PRICE STERN SLOAN

ROADSIDE AMUSEMENTS
an imprint of
CHAMBERLAIN BROS.
Published by the Penguin Group
Price Stern Sloan, a division of Penguin Group for Young Readers
Penguin Group (USA) Inc., 375 Hudson Street, New York, New York 10014, USA
Penguin Group (Canada), 90 Eglinton Avenue East, Suite 700,
Toronto, Ontario M4P 2Y3, Canada
(a division of Pearson Penguin Canada Inc.)
Penguin Books Ltd, 80 Strand, London WC2R 0RL, England
Penguin Ireland, 25 St Stephen's Green, Dublin 2, Ireland (a division of Penguin Books Ltd)
Penguin Group (Australia), 250 Camberwell Road, Camberwell, Victoria 3124, Australia
(a division of Pearson Australia Group Pty Ltd)
Penguin Books India Pvt Ltd, 11 Community Centre, Panchsheel Park,
New Delhi—110 017, India
Penguin Group (NZ), Cnr Airborne and Rosedale Roads,
Albany, Auckland 1310, New Zealand (a division of Pearson New Zealand Ltd)
Penguin Books (South Africa) (Pty) Ltd, 24 Sturdee Avenue,
Rosebank, Johannesburg 2196, South Africa

Penguin Books Ltd, Registered Offices: 80 Strand, London WC2R 0RL, England

Published simultaneously in Canada

An application has been submitted to register this book with the Library of Congress.

ISBN 1-59609-181-9

Printed in the United States of America
1 3 5 7 9 10 8 6 4 2

INSTRUCTIONS

MAD LIBS® is a game for people who don't like games! It can be played by one, two, three, four, or forty.

• RIDICULOUSLY SIMPLE DIRECTIONS

In this tablet you will find stories containing blank spaces where words are left out. One player, the **READER**, selects one of these stories. The **READER** does not tell anyone what the story is about. Instead, he/she asks the other players, the **WRITERS**, to give him/her words. These words are used to fill in the blank spaces in the story.

• TO PLAY

The **READER** asks each **WRITER** in turn to call out a word—an adjective or a noun or whatever the space calls for—and uses them to fill in the blank spaces in the story. The result is a **MAD LIBS®** game.

When the **READER** then reads the completed **MAD LIBS®** game to the other players, they will discover that they have written a story that is fantastic, screamingly funny, shocking, silly, crazy, or just plain dumb—depending upon which words each **WRITER** called out.

• EXAMPLE (*Before* and *After*)

"________________ (EXCLAMATION) !" he said ________________ (ADVERB)

as he jumped into his convertible ________________ (NOUN) and

drove off with his ________________ (ADJECTIVE) wife.

"Ouch (EXCLAMATION) !" he said stupidly (ADVERB)

as he jumped into his convertible cat (NOUN) and

drove off with his brave (ADJECTIVE) wife.

QUICK REVIEW

In case you have forgotten what adjectives, adverbs, nouns, and verbs are, here is a quick review:

An **ADJECTIVE** describes something or somebody. *Lumpy, soft, ugly, messy,* and *short* are adjectives.

An **ADVERB** tells how something is done. It modifies a verb and usually ends in "ly." *Modestly, stupidly, greedily,* and *carefully* are adverbs.

A **NOUN** is the name of a person, place, or thing. *Sidewalk, umbrella, bridle, bathtub,* and *nose* are nouns.

A **VERB** is an action word. *Run, pitch, jump,* and *swim* are verbs. Put the verbs in past tense if the directions say PAST TENSE. *Ran, pitched, jumped,* and *swam* are verbs in the past tense.

When we ask for **A PLACE**, we mean any sort of place: a country or city *(Spain, Cleveland)* or a room *(bathroom, kitchen).*

An **EXCLAMATION** or **SILLY WORD** is any sort of funny sound, gasp, grunt, or outcry, like *Wow!, Ouch!, Whomp!, Ick!,* and *Gadzooks!*

When we ask for specific words, like a **NUMBER**, a **COLOR**, an **ANIMAL**, or a **PART OF THE BODY**, we mean a word that is one of those things, like *seven, blue, horse,* or *head.*

When we ask for a **PLURAL**, it means more than one. For example, *cat* pluralized is *cats.*

MAD LIBS® is fun to play with friends, but you can also play it by yourself! To begin with, DO NOT look at the story on the page below. Fill in the blanks on this page with the words called for. Then, using the words you have selected, fill in the blank spaces in the story.

Now you've created your own hilarious MAD LIBS® game!

QUIZ

NOUN ______________________

ADJECTIVE ______________________

NOUN ______________________

NOUN ______________________

NOUN ______________________

VERB ______________________

NOUN ______________________

ADJECTIVE ______________________

ADJECTIVE ______________________

NOUN ______________________

MAD LIBS® QUIZ

How does one know if one's ________________ is dysfunctional?
NOUN

Here's a/an ________________ quiz to help you find out:
ADJECTIVE

1. Has a/an ________________ ever ignored you for months at a time?
NOUN

2. Do you already know that a certain ________________ will
NOUN
make a pass at your older ________________ during the next
NOUN
family gathering?

3. Did your parents ever ________________ in public?
VERB

4. Are you afraid to introduce your ________________ to your
NOUN
mother, for fear of being embarrassed?

If you answered yes to any of these ________________ questions,
ADJECTIVE
then the Cleavers you're not. Counseling may help to make you feel
________________, but at this stage you may just prefer a nice
ADJECTIVE
________________ lobotomy.
NOUN

MAD LIBS® is fun to play with friends, but you can also play it by yourself! To begin with, DO NOT look at the story on the page below. Fill in the blanks on this page with the words called for. Then, using the words you have selected, fill in the blank spaces in the story.

Now you've created your own hilarious MAD LIBS® game!

LONG CAR RIDES

NOUN ______________________

NOUN ______________________

ADVERB ______________________

NOUN ______________________

PERSON IN ROOM (FEMALE) ______________________

ADJECTIVE ______________________

NOUN ______________________

NOUN ______________________

VERB ENDING IN "ING" ______________________

NOUN ______________________

ADJECTIVE ______________________

PART OF THE BODY ______________________

NOUN ______________________

MAD LIBS®

LONG CAR RIDES

While driving along the interstate ____________ (NOUN), my sister starts poking me with her ____________ (NOUN). When I ask her to stop, she says ____________ (ADVERB), "You can't tell me what to do. You're not my ____________ (NOUN)." So I say, "Mom, will you please tell ____________ (PERSON IN ROOM (FEMALE)) to stop poking me?" But my mother ignores my ____________ (ADJECTIVE) plea. "Dad?" I appeal to the king of the ____________ (NOUN). He turns around with a big ____________ (NOUN) on his face and warns, "If you kids don't knock it off and stop ____________ (VERB ENDING IN "ING"), I will turn this ____________ (NOUN) around and head right back home!" After a moment of ____________ (ADJECTIVE) silence, my sister whispers into my ____________ (PART OF THE BODY), "Look what you did. Now we're going to have a terrible ____________ (NOUN)!"

MAD LIBS® is fun to play with friends, but you can also play it by yourself! To begin with, DO NOT look at the story on the page below. Fill in the blanks on this page with the words called for. Then, using the words you have selected, fill in the blank spaces in the story.

Now you've created your own hilarious MAD LIBS® game!

CASE HISTORY: THE SPOILED CHILD

PLURAL NOUN ____________

ADJECTIVE ____________

GEOGRAPHIC LOCATION ____________

NOUN ____________

NOUN ____________

VERB (PAST TENSE) ____________

NOUN ____________

ADJECTIVE ____________

SMALL CITY ____________

ADJECTIVE ____________

NOUN ____________

PLURAL NOUN ____________

NOUN ____________

NOUN ____________

MAD LIBS®
CASE HISTORY: THE SPOILED CHILD

Spoiled children constantly demand new ________ (PLURAL NOUN) to play with, as they are never satisfied with what they have. History's most ________ (ADJECTIVE) example is Henry VIII. Discontented with his first wife, Catherine of ________ (GEOGRAPHIC LOCATION), Henry divorced her and wed Anne Boleyn. But she had a melancholy ________ (NOUN), so he executed her. His next ________ (NOUN), Jane Seymour, ________ (VERB (PAST TENSE)) while giving birth, which made Henry cry like a/an ________ (NOUN). He got over it by ordering a new bride from a/an ________ (ADJECTIVE) country. Unfortunately, when Anne of ________ (SMALL CITY) arrived, Henry screamed that he found her to be too ________ (ADJECTIVE), so he set her aside and married Katherine Howard. However, she cheated on him so he chopped off her ________ (NOUN). Finally, there was Catherine Parr, the last of his ________ (PLURAL NOUN), who survived him. Henry was a spoiled ________ (NOUN) who grew up to become an even more spoiled ________ (NOUN). Someone should have administered a royal time-out!

MAD LIBS® is fun to play with friends, but you can also play it by yourself! To begin with, DO NOT look at the story on the page below. Fill in the blanks on this page with the words called for. Then, using the words you have selected, fill in the blank spaces in the story.

Now you've created your own hilarious MAD LIBS® game!

FUN FAMILY PICNIC

NOUN ________________

ADJECTIVE ________________

NOUN ________________

NOUN ________________

NOUN ________________

NOUN ________________

NOUN ________________

VERB ________________

NOUN ________________

NOUN ________________

PLURAL NOUN ________________

NOUN ________________

PART OF THE BODY ________________

ADVERB ________________

PART OF THE BODY (PLURAL) ________________

PLURAL NOUN ________________

ADJECTIVE ________________

NOUN ________________

PLURAL NOUN ________________

NOUN ________________

MAD LIBS®

FUN FAMILY PICNIC

As usual, our family ________________ (NOUN) was a/an ________________ (ADJECTIVE) disaster. Mom packed ____________ (NOUN) sandwiches and ____________ (NOUN) salad, and Dad brought a volleyball and a/an ________________ (NOUN). Once we got to the ________________ (NOUN) grounds, my brother started shooting me with a water ________________ (NOUN). But when I screamed, "________________ (VERB)!" my mom got mad and said, "You just calm down, young ________________ (NOUN)." Dad was having some trouble setting up the ________________ (NOUN) net, so I offered to help, but he shouted at the top of his ________________ (PLURAL NOUN), "Just stay out of the ________________ (NOUN)!" Then I went to give a/an ________________ (PART OF THE BODY) to Mom. "Well, it's about time somebody offered to help," she said ____________ (ADVERB), and then rolled her ________________ (PART OF THE BODY (PLURAL)). I spent the rest of the day eating Mom's ________________ (PLURAL NOUN) (which had become ____________ (ADJECTIVE) in the sun) and watching Dad fight with the ____________ (NOUN). I wish we could be more like normal ____________ (PLURAL NOUN) and spend weekends watching reruns on the ____________ (NOUN).

MAD LIBS® is fun to play with friends, but you can also play it by yourself! To begin with, DO NOT look at the story on the page below. Fill in the blanks on this page with the words called for. Then, using the words you have selected, fill in the blank spaces in the story.

Now you've created your own hilarious MAD LIBS® game!

THE BRADY BUNCH

NOUN ____________

PLURAL NOUN ____________

OCCUPATION ____________

NOUN ____________

ANIMAL ____________

NOUN ____________

PLURAL NOUN ____________

NOUN ____________

ADJECTIVE ____________

NOUN ____________

OCCUPATION ____________

NOUN ____________

VERB ____________

ADJECTIVE ____________

PLURAL NOUN ____________

NOUN ____________

NOUN ____________

ADJECTIVE ____________

MAD LIBS®

THE BRADY BUNCH

Growing up, I envied the Brady ____________ (NOUN). Carol and Mike Brady each had three ____________ (PLURAL NOUN), plus a/an ____________ (OCCUPATION) and a/an ____________ (NOUN) named ____________ (ANIMAL). They all lived together as one big, happy ____________ (NOUN). (I can still remember their silly ____________ (PLURAL NOUN) clear as a/an ____________ (NOUN).) On one ____________ (ADJECTIVE) episode, Jan bought a/an ____________ (NOUN) and actually wore it to a party. On another, Marcia developed a crush on her ____________ (OCCUPATION). And who can forget the time the kids broke Mom's favorite ____________ (NOUN) and tried to ____________ (VERB) it back together? In the end, Carol and Mike always learned the truth and taught the kids a/an ____________ (ADJECTIVE) lesson. Mike said, "You know, when you tell on your ____________ (PLURAL NOUN), you're really telling on yourself," and "You have to learn to keep a/an ____________ (NOUN)—nobody likes a tattle____________ (NOUN)." Such ____________ (ADJECTIVE) wisdom!

MAD LIBS® is fun to play with friends, but you can also play it by yourself! To begin with, DO NOT look at the story on the page below. Fill in the blanks on this page with the words called for. Then, using the words you have selected, fill in the blank spaces in the story.

Now you've created your own hilarious MAD LIBS® game!

THANKSGIVING DAY SURVIVAL

NOUN ____________________

ADJECTIVE ____________________

NOUN ____________________

NOUN ____________________

NOUN ____________________

NOUN ____________________

PLURAL NOUN ____________________

NUMBER ____________________

ADJECTIVE ____________________

NOUN ____________________

NOUN ____________________

NUMBER ____________________

PLURAL NOUN ____________________

ADJECTIVE ____________________

MAD LIBS®

THANKSGIVING DAY SURVIVAL

Thanksgiving with your ____________ (NOUN) can be a/an ____________ (ADJECTIVE) experience, but you've got to come prepared. Don't just show up at your parents' ____________ (NOUN) expecting everything to be peaches 'n' ____________ (NOUN). Make a plan. To participate, first go to the kitchen and help your mother cook the gigantic ____________ (NOUN) she bought. Then greet each individual ____________ (NOUN) at the door, take their ____________ (PLURAL NOUN), and seat them at least ____________ (NUMBER) feet away from each other. Start the conversation by asking Dad about his ____________ (ADJECTIVE) old days as the ____________ (NOUN) of his high-school ____________ (NOUN) team. (Anything to make him forget that you still owe ____________ (NUMBER) dollars for your tuition.) It will also keep your grandparents from talking, thus sparing you the lecture on the "outrageous price of ____________ (PLURAL NOUN) these days." Finally—and please don't overlook this very ____________ (ADJECTIVE) step—bring proof that you looked for a job in the past week!

MAD LIBS® is fun to play with friends, but you can also play it by yourself! To begin with, DO NOT look at the story on the page below. Fill in the blanks on this page with the words called for. Then, using the words you have selected, fill in the blank spaces in the story.

Now you've created your own hilarious MAD LIBS® game!

MOTHER, MAY I?

PERSON IN ROOM ____________________

EXCLAMATION ____________________

ADJECTIVE ____________________

NOUN ____________________

NOUN ____________________

SAME NOUN ____________________

NOUN ____________________

NOUN ____________________

ADJECTIVE ____________________

NOUN ____________________

NOUN ____________________

ADJECTIVE ____________________

VERB ENDING IN "ING" ____________________

ADVERB ____________________

PLURAL NOUN ____________________

PERSON IN ROOM ____________________

NOUN ____________________

MAD LIBS®

MOTHER, MAY I?

________ (PERSON IN ROOM) asked if I wanted to sleep over and I said, "________ (EXCLAMATION)! That sounds ________ (ADJECTIVE). But I'll have to ask my ________ (NOUN) for permission." So I went to Mom and she said, "Go ask your ________ (NOUN)." So I asked my ________ (SAME NOUN) and he said, "Ask your ________ (NOUN)." Exasperated, I said, "Is anyone here capable of making a/an ________ (NOUN)?" Then Dad got mad and said, "Don't get ________ (ADJECTIVE) with me, young ________ (NOUN). Now go to your ________ (NOUN)." I complained to Mom that this wasn't fair, but she said, "Nobody said life was ________ (ADJECTIVE)." "Well, it should be!" I cried, but nobody was ________ (VERB ENDING IN "ING"). I dropped the subject and went away ________ (ADVERB), fighting back ________ (PLURAL NOUN). The next day, ________ (PERSON IN ROOM) called and asked me over for dinner. "Ask your ________ (NOUN)," my mother said....

MAD LIBS® is fun to play with friends, but you can also play it by yourself! To begin with, DO NOT look at the story on the page below. Fill in the blanks on this page with the words called for. Then, using the words you have selected, fill in the blank spaces in the story.

Now you've created your own hilarious MAD LIBS® game!

HOW TO INTRODUCE YOUR BOYFRIEND

ADJECTIVE ____________________

ADJECTIVE ____________________

ADJECTIVE ____________________

ADJECTIVE ____________________

NOUN ____________________

ADJECTIVE ____________________

PLURAL NOUN ____________________

NOUN ____________________

TYPE OF EVENT ____________________

NOUN ____________________

NOUN ____________________

NOUN ____________________

SAME NOUN ____________________

NOUN ____________________

MAD LIBS®

HOW TO INTRODUCE YOUR BOYFRIEND

Will your family scare your ________ (ADJECTIVE) new boyfriend away? Chances are ________ (ADJECTIVE) that they will, so you should take some ________ (ADJECTIVE) steps beforehand to ensure a/an ________ (ADJECTIVE) meeting:

1. Encourage your guy to bring a/an ________ (NOUN) for your mother. (This should guarantee a/an ________ (ADJECTIVE) first impression.)
2. If your family has any unusual ________ (PLURAL NOUN), warn your boyfriend ahead of time.
3. Tell your mother not to discuss your ex-________ (NOUN) and how devastated you were when he called off the ________ (TYPE OF EVENT) at the last ________ (NOUN).

Finally, don't panic. Your ________ (NOUN) will still love you. After all, he is not dating your ________ (NOUN), he's dating you. (And if he wishes he were dating your ________ (SAME NOUN), then maybe you should be looking for a new ________ (NOUN)!)

MAD LIBS® is fun to play with friends, but you can also play it by yourself! To begin with, DO NOT look at the story on the page below. Fill in the blanks on this page with the words called for. Then, using the words you have selected, fill in the blank spaces in the story.

Now you've created your own hilarious MAD LIBS® game!

CHRISTMAS

ADJECTIVE ______________________

ADJECTIVE ______________________

ADJECTIVE ______________________

PLURAL NOUN ______________________

NUMBER ______________________

ADJECTIVE ______________________

NOUN ______________________

ADVERB ______________________

PLURAL NOUN ______________________

ADJECTIVE ______________________

PLURAL NOUN ______________________

NUMBER ______________________

VERB ENDING IN "ING" ______________________

NOUN ______________________

PLURAL NOUN ______________________

ADJECTIVE ______________________

NOUN ______________________

SAME NOUN ______________________

SAME NOUN ______________________

MAD LIBS®

CHRISTMAS

Christmas gatherings require you to not only tolerate your ________ (ADJECTIVE) family's ________ (ADJECTIVE) company but also to exchange ________ (ADJECTIVE) ________ (PLURAL NOUN)! You have to spend ________ (NUMBER) months' salary on ________ (ADJECTIVE) presents and then smile and appear grateful when you receive another horrible ________ (NOUN) that only proves ________ (ADVERB) that none of your ________ (PLURAL NOUN) really know you at all. Your mother always buys you ________ (ADJECTIVE) pants and ________ (PLURAL NOUN) that are usually ________ (NUMBER) size(s) too small. Your father always gives you some sort of ________ (VERB ENDING IN "ING") kit that ends up collecting dust on the floor of your ________ (NOUN). The worst is your little brother, who buys you the latest video ________ (PLURAL NOUN) just so he can borrow them later on. Maybe this year you should make a/an ________ (ADJECTIVE) new rule: ________ (NOUN) certificates, ________ (SAME NOUN) certificates, ________ (SAME NOUN) certificates!

MAD LIBS® is fun to play with friends, but you can also play it by yourself! To begin with, DO NOT look at the story on the page below. Fill in the blanks on this page with the words called for. Then, using the words you have selected, fill in the blank spaces in the story.

Now you've created your own hilarious MAD LIBS® game!

CASE HISTORY: ANGER MANAGEMENT

ADJECTIVE ______________________

PLURAL NOUN ______________________

ADJECTIVE ______________________

NOUN ______________________

NATIONALITY ______________________

VERB (PAST TENSE) ______________________

PLURAL NOUN ______________________

ADJECTIVE ______________________

ADJECTIVE ______________________

ADJECTIVE ______________________

ADJECTIVE ______________________

PART OF THE BODY ______________________

NOUN ______________________

ADJECTIVE ______________________

MAD LIBS®
CASE HISTORY: ANGER MANAGEMENT

Alexander the Great was a/an ____________ (ADJECTIVE) candidate for anger management, because he employed ____________ (PLURAL NOUN) rather than diplomacy to solve problems. Here are a few ____________ (ADJECTIVE) examples:

1. A/An ____________ (NOUN) once refused to bow to Alexander in the ____________ (NATIONALITY) fashion, so Alexander had him killed.
2. Some governors ____________ (VERB (PAST TENSE)) during Alexander's absence, so he had them killed.
3. After exploring foreign ____________ (PLURAL NOUN) and meeting all kinds of new and ____________ (ADJECTIVE) people, he . . . well, you know!

One can't help but wonder what ____________ (ADJECTIVE) Alexander was so angry about—other than the fact that his parents were so ____________ (ADJECTIVE). But what I would like to know is: Once it became clear that young Alex had a/an ____________ (ADJECTIVE) chip on his ____________ (PART OF THE BODY) the size of a/an ____________ (NOUN), whose ____________ (ADJECTIVE) idea was it to give him his own army?

MAD LIBS® is fun to play with friends, but you can also play it by yourself! To begin with, DO NOT look at the story on the page below. Fill in the blanks on this page with the words called for. Then, using the words you have selected, fill in the blank spaces in the story.

Now you've created your own hilarious MAD LIBS® game!

FAMILY PLAN

VERB ______________________

NOUN ______________________

ADJECTIVE ______________________

NUMBER ______________________

ADJECTIVE ______________________

VERB ENDING IN "ING" ______________________

VERB (PAST TENSE) ______________________

ADJECTIVE ______________________

NOUN ______________________

ADJECTIVE ______________________

NOUN ______________________

PLURAL NOUN ______________________

NOUN ______________________

NOUN ______________________

ADJECTIVE ______________________

NOUN ______________________

MAD LIBS®

FAMILY PLAN

Well, we bought the "Family ____________ Plan" from our
VERB
mobile ____________ company. ____________ mistake!
NOUN ADJECTIVE
At just ____________ cents a minute, it seemed like a/an
NUMBER
____________ idea. The first call was from my sister saying
ADJECTIVE
she didn't make the ____________ squad at school. She then
VERB ENDING IN "ING"
____________ for an hour while I was trying to watch my
VERB (PAST TENSE)
____________ TV show, *American* ____________. Then
ADJECTIVE NOUN
my phone rang again and it was my ____________ brother,
ADJECTIVE
asking me to pick him up from ____________ practice. On
NOUN
the way home, my mother called and asked me to pick up some
____________ at the neighborhood ____________, and
PLURAL NOUN NOUN
my father called asking where the car was because he had to get to a
very important ____________ by six o'clock! I think I might "lose"
NOUN
my ____________ phone tomorrow and tell the company what
ADJECTIVE
they can do with their "Family ____________"!
NOUN

MAD LIBS® is fun to play with friends, but you can also play it by yourself! To begin with, DO NOT look at the story on the page below. Fill in the blanks on this page with the words called for. Then, using the words you have selected, fill in the blank spaces in the story.

Now you've created your own hilarious MAD LIBS® game!

THINGS MOM ALWAYS SAID

ADJECTIVE ____________________

NOUN ____________________

PLURAL NOUN ____________________

NOUN ____________________

ADJECTIVE ____________________

VERB (PAST TENSE) ____________________

PLURAL NOUN ____________________

NOUN ____________________

NOUN ____________________

NOUN ____________________

NOUN ____________________

ADJECTIVE ____________________

PLURAL NOUN ____________________

MAD LIBS®

THINGS MOM ALWAYS SAID

These are some of the ____________ (ADJECTIVE) phrases you might, unfortunately, remember hearing from your mother's ____________ (NOUN):

- "Well, if the other ____________ (PLURAL NOUN) jumped off the Brooklyn ____________ (NOUN), would you do it, too?"
- "Always wear ____________ (ADJECTIVE) underwear in case you're in an accident."
- "I never ____________ (VERB (PAST TENSE)) when I was your age."
- "Turn on the ____________ (PLURAL NOUN) when you read—you'll go blind."
- "Don't sit so close to the ____________ (NOUN)—you'll go blind."
- "Don't use your ____________ (NOUN) to wipe your face. Always have a clean ____________ (NOUN) with you."
- "Put on a warm ____________ (NOUN)—you'll catch cold.

I guess when I'm older, I'll impart the same ____________ (ADJECTIVE) wisdom to my ____________ (PLURAL NOUN).

MAD LIBS® is fun to play with friends, but you can also play it by yourself! To begin with, DO NOT look at the story on the page below. Fill in the blanks on this page with the words called for. Then, using the words you have selected, fill in the blank spaces in the story.

Now you've created your own hilarious MAD LIBS® game!

MOM'S MEAT LOAF

NUMBER ____________________

NOUN ____________________

ADJECTIVE ____________________

NOUN ____________________

ADVERB ____________________

NOUN ____________________

PLURAL NOUN ____________________

NOUN ____________________

NUMBER ____________________

NUMBER ____________________

ADJECTIVE ____________________

PLURAL NOUN ____________________

ADJECTIVE ____________________

NOUN ____________________

PLURAL NOUN ____________________

NOUN ____________________

MAD LIBS®

MOM'S MEAT LOAF

Ah . . . home cookin'. Here's how to make meat loaf exactly like Mom's:

1. In a bowl, combine ________ (NUMBER) eggs, a pound of chopped ________ (NOUN), ________ (ADJECTIVE) salt, ________ (NOUN) paste, and mustard.
2. Crumble meat over the mixture and mix ________ (ADVERB). Sprinkle with onion and ________ (NOUN) crumbs. Mix again and then shape into two ________ (PLURAL NOUN).
3. Place loaves in the center of a lightly floured ________ (NOUN).
4. Bake at ________ (NUMBER) degrees for ________ (NUMBER) minutes or until thoroughly ________ (ADJECTIVE).
5. For the sauce, take some melted ________ (PLURAL NOUN) and whisk in flour until it's completely ________ (ADJECTIVE). Stir in one ________ (NOUN) and two ________ (PLURAL NOUN). If you like, you can substitute a/an ________ (NOUN) for the flour.

Finally, when your children refuse to eat your creation, storm out of the room and shout, "Nobody appreciates me!"

MAD LIBS® is fun to play with friends, but you can also play it by yourself! To begin with, DO NOT look at the story on the page below. Fill in the blanks on this page with the words called for. Then, using the words you have selected, fill in the blank spaces in the story.

Now you've created your own hilarious MAD LIBS® game!

THE DYSFUNCTIONAL FAMILY MOVIE

NOUN ____________________

PLURAL NOUN ____________________

PERSON IN ROOM (MALE) ____________________

CELEBRITY (MALE) ____________________

NOUN ____________________

PLURAL NOUN ____________________

ADJECTIVE ____________________

GEOGRAPHIC LOCATION ____________________

CELEBRITY (FEMALE) ____________________

PART OF THE BODY ____________________

NOUN ____________________

PART OF THE BODY ____________________

PLURAL NOUN ____________________

MAD LIBS®

THE DYSFUNCTIONAL FAMILY MOVIE

The ________________ *in Winter* features a dysfunctional family of
NOUN

royal ________________. The year is 1183 and the film centers
PLURAL NOUN

on King ________________ the Second, played by
PERSON IN ROOM (MALE)

________________, who must decide which of his sons will
CELEBRITY (MALE)

take over his royal ________________. He summons the three
NOUN

________________, who are all extremely greedy, evil, and
PLURAL NOUN

________________. But even worse is their mother, Queen Eleanor
ADJECTIVE

of ________________, played by ________________, who
GEOGRAPHIC LOCATION CELEBRITY (FEMALE)

has a/an ________________ of stone. She's especially angry at the
PART OF THE BODY

king because he (1) threw her in prison, and (2) had an affair with

a/an ________________ behind her ________________! It's
NOUN PART OF THE BODY

a relief to know that modern royal families don't have to deal with

________________ like these anymore . . . er, never mind!
PLURAL NOUN

MAD LIBS® is fun to play with friends, but you can also play it by yourself! To begin with, DO NOT look at the story on the page below. Fill in the blanks on this page with the words called for. Then, using the words you have selected, fill in the blank spaces in the story.

Now you've created your own hilarious MAD LIBS® game!

TALKING

PLURAL NOUN ______________________

NOUN ______________________

ADVERB ______________________

ADJECTIVE ______________________

ADJECTIVE ______________________

NOUN ______________________

NUMBER ______________________

ADJECTIVE ______________________

NOUN ______________________

ADJECTIVE ______________________

NOUN ______________________

NOUN ______________________

NOUN ______________________

MAD LIBS®

TALKING

Talking is something that dysfunctional ________________ should
PLURAL NOUN

never attempt to do, but there are times when it cannot be avoided,

such as at a family ________________. The secret to getting through
NOUN

one of these "get-togethers" is to tell everyone how you are without

________________ giving away any ________________ information.
ADVERB / ADJECTIVE

(That way, nothing too ________________ can get back to your mother.)
ADJECTIVE

You are obligated to chat with each ________________ for only
NOUN

________________ minutes, and then it's considered ________________
NUMBER / ADJECTIVE

to take your leave and escape to the next ________________. First,
NOUN

make sure the television is on, if possible, to break the ________________
ADJECTIVE

silence. When you see your aunt, compliment her on her new

________________ and ask where she got it. Finally, prepare an
NOUN

emergency phrase, in case someone asks about your ________________ —
NOUN

something like, "Does anyone know who got eliminated on *American*

________________ last night?"
NOUN

MAD LIBS® is fun to play with friends, but you can also play it by yourself! To begin with, DO NOT look at the story on the page below. Fill in the blanks on this page with the words called for. Then, using the words you have selected, fill in the blank spaces in the story.

Now you've created your own hilarious MAD LIBS® game!

SCHOOL COUNSELOR

NOUN ____________

NOUN ____________

PLURAL NOUN ____________

ADJECTIVE ____________

PLURAL NOUN ____________

ADJECTIVE ____________

PLURAL NOUN ____________

PERSON IN ROOM (FEMALE) ____________

NOUN ____________

PART OF THE BODY ____________

PLURAL NOUN ____________

ADJECTIVE ____________

NOUN ____________

NUMBER ____________

NOUN ____________

NOUN ____________

MAD LIBS®

SCHOOL COUNSELOR

Throughout my thirty-year career as a high-school guidance __________ (NOUN), I've worked with just about every kind of dysfunctional __________ (NOUN). I've seen teenagers act like spoiled __________ (PLURAL NOUN) just to get attention, I've seen __________ (ADJECTIVE) children with neurotic __________ (PLURAL NOUN), and I've seen __________ (ADJECTIVE) things happen to good __________ (PLURAL NOUN). My greatest success story involved a young lady named __________ (PERSON IN THE ROOM (FEMALE)), who was what we in the business call a/an "__________ (NOUN)-maniac." (She had a kind __________ (PART OF THE BODY), but her self-definition was centered entirely on __________ (PLURAL NOUN).) With her __________ (ADJECTIVE) behavior patterns, I was afraid she would end up in what we call a "Vicious __________ (NOUN)." I worked with her for __________ (NUMBER) years, teaching her to value her __________ (NOUN) more. Eventually she grew up to become a strong, independent __________ (NOUN)…. And now she doesn't return my phone calls.

MAD LIBS® is fun to play with friends, but you can also play it by yourself! To begin with, DO NOT look at the story on the page below. Fill in the blanks on this page with the words called for. Then, using the words you have selected, fill in the blank spaces in the story.

Now you've created your own hilarious MAD LIBS® game!

SKI VACATION

ADJECTIVE ____________________

ADJECTIVE ____________________

NOUN ____________________

PLURAL NOUN ____________________

NOUN ____________________

NOUN ____________________

NOUN ____________________

NOUN ____________________

ADJECTIVE ____________________

NOUN ____________________

NOUN ____________________

NOUN ____________________

NOUN ____________________

MAD LIBS®

SKI VACATION

None of us had ever gone skiing before, but Dad insisted that it was ____________ (ADJECTIVE) fun and we were going to have a/an ____________ (ADJECTIVE) weekend. I've heard that before. We spent the first day in the shops because Mom wanted to look like a/an ____________ (NOUN) on the slopes. The second day, she went back because she forgot to buy ____________ (PLURAL NOUN) to go with her new ____________ (NOUN), so Dad and I left without her. At the foot of the mountain, our car got a flat ____________ (NOUN) and we waited four hours for an auto ____________ (NOUN) truck to come along. By the time the ____________ (NOUN) was fixed, we were too ____________ (ADJECTIVE) to go skiing, so we just went back to the hotel and took a/an ____________ (NOUN). On the last day, the ____________ (NOUN) came out and melted all the snow. Dad's face turned as red as a/an ____________ (NOUN). Next year, Mom says we're going someplace warm. She's already shopping for a new ____________ (NOUN)!

MAD LIBS® is fun to play with friends, but you can also play it by yourself! To begin with, DO NOT look at the story on the page below. Fill in the blanks on this page with the words called for. Then, using the words you have selected, fill in the blank spaces in the story.

Now you've created your own hilarious MAD LIBS® game!

SUPERNANNY

NOUN ____________________

NOUN ____________________

CELEBRITY (FEMALE) ____________________

PLURAL NOUN ____________________

PLURAL NOUN ____________________

ADJECTIVE ____________________

ADJECTIVE ____________________

ADJECTIVE ____________________

NOUN ____________________

A PLACE ____________________

PLURAL NOUN ____________________

ADJECTIVE ____________________

NOUN ____________________

NOUN ____________________

ADJECTIVE ____________________

MAD LIBS®

SUPERNANNY

Television's newest ________________ can get the most difficult
NOUN

________________ to overcome problems that have plagued
NOUN

parents since the beginning of time. In each episode of *Supernanny*,

________________ works with children to correct their bad
CELEBRITY (FEMALE)

________________. She begins by explaining that she'd like them
PLURAL NOUN

to follow some new ________________. Then she proceeds to
PLURAL NOUN

reward ________________ behavior and punish ________________
ADJECTIVE ADJECTIVE

behavior. One ________________ punishment is a short time-out
ADJECTIVE

on the "Naughty ________________" or, for older children, in the
NOUN

"Naughty ________________"—a place without ________________
A PLACE PLURAL NOUN

or TV. The children's behavior grows more ________________ with
ADJECTIVE

each passing day, and eventually the desired ________________ is
NOUN

achieved! *Supernanny* is ridding the world of behavioral dysfunction,

one ________________ at a time. Too bad our ________________ parents
NOUN ADJECTIVE

missed the cut and we turned out this way!

MAD LIBS® is fun to play with friends, but you can also play it by yourself! To begin with, DO NOT look at the story on the page below. Fill in the blanks on this page with the words called for. Then, using the words you have selected, fill in the blank spaces in the story.

Now you've created your own hilarious MAD LIBS® game!

CASE HISTORY: CONTROLLING MOTHER

VERB (PAST TENSE) ____________________

NOUN ____________________

ADJECTIVE ____________________

NOUN ____________________

ADJECTIVE ____________________

PLURAL NOUN ____________________

ADJECTIVE ____________________

NOUN ____________________

NOUN ____________________

PART OF THE BODY ____________________

ADJECTIVE ____________________

NOUN ____________________

MAD LIBS®

CASE HISTORY: CONTROLLING MOTHER

Agrippina ____________ from A.D. 15 to A.D. 59. She
VERB (PAST TENSE)

was clearly one of history's first "Controlling Mothers" because she

was always telling little Nero how to run the ____________.
NOUN

As he matured, Nero became ____________ and decided to
ADJECTIVE

have his mother moved to a/an ____________ far away. But
NOUN

this didn't stop Agrippina's ____________ ways, so Nero
ADJECTIVE

employed more extreme ____________ to get rid of her. First
PLURAL NOUN

he tried poison, but it didn't work because she was ____________
ADJECTIVE

enough to take a/an ____________ beforehand. Next, he tried
NOUN

to rig the ____________ in her bedchamber to fall on her
NOUN

____________ while she slept, but that never works. Growing
PART OF THE BODY

desperate, he sent her out to sea in a/an ____________
ADJECTIVE

boat with a leaky ____________, but she swam to safety.
NOUN

Nero finally gave up and became an actor, which those of us with

controlling mothers know is about all you can really do . . . .

MAD LIBS® is fun to play with friends, but you can also play it by yourself! To begin with, DO NOT look at the story on the page below. Fill in the blanks on this page with the words called for. Then, using the words you have selected, fill in the blank spaces in the story.

Now you've created your own hilarious MAD LIBS® game!

LIFE COACHING

NOUN ________________

NOUN ________________

NOUN ________________

PLURAL NOUN ________________

NOUN ________________

NOUN ________________

ADJECTIVE ________________

NOUN ________________

NOUN ________________

VERB ENDING IN "ING" ________________

ADJECTIVE ________________

ADVERB ________________

NOUN ________________

PLURAL NOUN ________________

NOUN ________________

PLURAL NOUN ________________

MAD LIBS®

LIFE COACHING

Coaching is a partnership between a/an ________________ and
NOUN

a/an ________________ that is designed to help a dysfunctional
NOUN

young ________________ reach his or her ________________. It
NOUN PLURAL NOUN

is a step-by-________________ process that creates clarity and
NOUN

________________-filled moments. Here are some of the mental,
NOUN

emotional, and ________________ benefits of coaching:
ADJECTIVE

- Discovering your inner ________________ and allowing it to play
  NOUN
- Recovering from a traumatic ________________
  NOUN
- Learning the art of "________________"
  VERB ENDING IN "ING"
- Learning how to change ________________ thinking
  ADJECTIVE
- Learning how to protect yourself ________________
  ADVERB

The relationship between a/an ________________ and a coach
NOUN

transforms ________________. Too bad it costs more money than
PLURAL NOUN

you can shake a/an ________________ at. Maybe you could try
NOUN

squeezing one of those nice stress ________________ instead?
PLURAL NOUN

MAD LIBS® is fun to play with friends, but you can also play it by yourself! To begin with, DO NOT look at the story on the page below. Fill in the blanks on this page with the words called for. Then, using the words you have selected, fill in the blank spaces in the story.

Now you've created your own hilarious MAD LIBS® game!

DATING AFTER DIVORCE

VERB ____________________

NUMBER ____________________

ADJECTIVE ____________________

ADJECTIVE ____________________

ADJECTIVE ____________________

PLURAL NOUN ____________________

NOUN ____________________

PART OF THE BODY ____________________

PLURAL NOUN ____________________

NOUN ____________________

PLURAL NOUN ____________________

NOUN ____________________

VERB ENDING IN "ING" ____________________

ADJECTIVE ____________________

NOUN ____________________

MAD LIBS®

DATING AFTER DIVORCE

It's been a few months since the divorce and you're ready to ____________ (VERB) again. Whether you're forty or ____________ (NUMBER), dating might feel completely ____________ (ADJECTIVE). Here are a few tips to help you ease back into the ____________ (ADJECTIVE) scene:

1. Don't try to look too ____________ (ADJECTIVE). If you arc fifty ____________ (PLURAL NOUN) or older, do not walk into a/an ____________ (NOUN) club frequented by nineteen-year-olds. You will stand out like a sore ____________ (PART OF THE BODY).
2. Keep ____________ (PLURAL NOUN) short. It creates a sense of mystery.
3. Do not, under any circumstances, talk about your cx-____________ (NOUN).
4. Explore new ____________ (PLURAL NOUN). Consider using a/an ____________ (NOUN) agency or visiting a/an ____________ (VERB ENDING IN "ING") Web site. It might sound ____________ (ADJECTIVE), but anything is worth trying at least once, right? Now get out there and find yourself that new ____________ (NOUN)...or at least a new dog!

Adult

MAD LIBS®

World's Greatest Word Game

Roger Price and Leonard Stern

Look for these fun Adult Mad Libs® titles at a bookseller near you!

ADVICE FOR THE LOVELORN

Dumper? Dumpee? Who's sorry now? This compilation of advice column wisdom, Dear John letters, old love notes, and other comforts is for those tortured souls left in the lurch whose friends simply don't want to hear about it anymore.

TEST YOUR RELATIONSHIP I.Q.

Take the tests and find out if you're a match made in heaven…or doomed to a life of utter boredom and marital horror!

KEEPERS AND LOSERS

A rating guide of men: smarts, looks, stamina, charm, manners, and other lists to rate whether you should bring him home to Mom or throw him back into the sea.

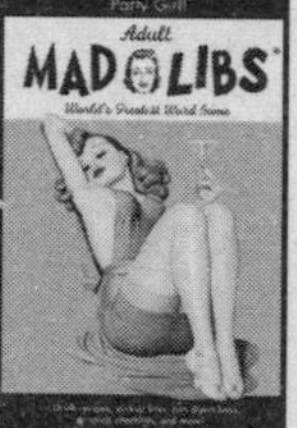

PARTY GIRL

Drink recipes, pickup lines, turndown lines, chick checklists, and more.

DYSFUNCTIONAL FAMILY THERAPY

Holiday memories. Mom's advice. All that quality time. *Dysfunctional Family Therapy* addresses all the reasons you can never go home again.

BACHELORETTE BASH

Congratulations, you're getting married! And whether you're organizing the wedding of the century or planning to elope, every bride-to-be deserves that one last night with the girls. *Adult Mad Libs®* leads the fun with checklists, games, Guest Confidentiality Agreements, and much, much more. . . .